Tales of the TINY FOLK

Published by Stone Arch Books, an imprint of Capstone
1710 Roe Crest Drive, North Mankato, Minnesota 56003
capstonepub.com

Library of Congress Cataloging-in-Publication Data
Names: Foxe, Steve, author. | Barros, Daniela (Illustrator), illustrator.
Title: Iggy follows the snail trail / written by Steve Foxe ; illustrated by Daniela Barros.
Description: North Mankato, Minnesota : Stone Arch Books, an imprint of Capstone, [2024]. | Series: Tales of the Tiny Folk | Audience: Ages 7-11. | Audience: Grades 4-6. | Summary: When Iggy's pet snail wanders away, Iggy must face his fears and follow the slimy trail which leads into the wild woods.
Identifiers: LCCN 2023038702 (print) | LCCN 2023038703 (ebook) | ISBN 9781669059899 (hardcover) | ISBN 9781669060024 (paperback) | ISBN 9781669059967 (pdf) | ISBN 9781669060031 (epub) | ISBN 9781669060048 (kindle edition)
Subjects: LCSH: Snails—Comic books, strips, etc. | Snails—Juvenile fiction. | Pets—Comic books, strips, etc. | Pets—Juvenile fiction. | Fear—Comic books, strips, etc. | Fear—Juvenile fiction. | CYAC: Graphic novels. | Snails—Fiction. | Pets—Fiction. | Fear—Fiction. | LCGFT: Fantasy comics. | Graphic novels.
Classification: LCC PZ7.7.F69 Ig 2024 (print) | LCC PZ7.7.F69 (ebook) | DDC 741.5/973—dc23/eng/20230828
LC record available at https://lccn.loc.gov/2023038702
LC ebook record available at https://lccn.loc.gov/2023038703

Designed by Hilary Wacholz
Edited by Abby Huff

Printed and bound in the USA. 5626

Tales of the Tiny Folk

Iggy Follows the Snail Trail

Written by Steve Foxe
Illustrated by Daniela Barros

STONE ARCH BOOKS
a capstone imprint

Hey! Down here!

Bet you've never noticed us before, huh? We are the Tiny Folk.

You know all the stuff you drop around the house, or that falls out of your backpack? The pencils, buttons, paper clips, rubber bands, and hair ties you lose? We turn those things into our houses, tools, and clothes!

Us Tiny Folk live in your gardens and yards, just out of sight. We grow itty-bitty plants, make friends with bugs and little animals, and enjoy our tiny lives on the edge of nature.

But sometimes Tiny Folk go on BIG adventures. When we help each other, no challenge is too large!

Slimy! Breakfast time!
Come and get it, big guy.

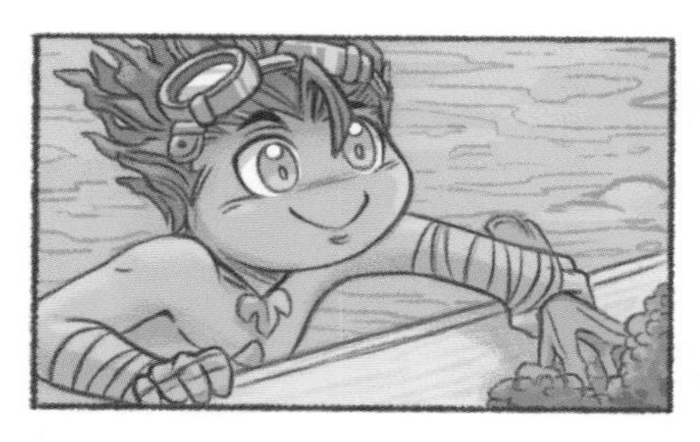

Wow...

...you're moving fast today, Slimy!

Wanna go for a walk? I don't have any—
CRUNCH
Agh, wait! I promised to help Kora clean moss off her roof!

I'll be back real soon, okay?
CREEEEAK

An hour later . . .
Thanks again for your help, Iggy.
No sweat, Kora!
Now, I owe Slimy a...

...walk.
SMAK
SMAK

Oh no! I was in such a hurry that I must not have latched the gate.

Where are you, Slimy?
Slimy?!

I don't see him anywhere, Ig.

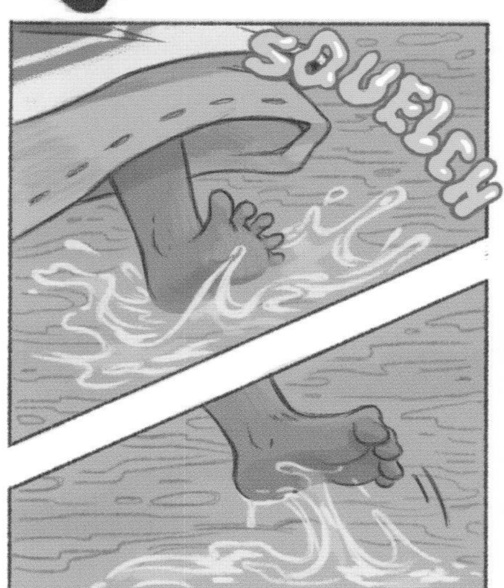
SQUELCH

Ugh, what did I step in?

You found Slimy's trail!
And it leads...

...into the woods.
With all the big animals that like to eat smaller animals.
gulp

Don't panic, Ig. We can put together a search party and—
That'll take too long. I am going to look for Slimy.
Before he wanders deeper into the woods.

Stay here in case he comes back?
Of course. Be safe.

Oh! Iggy, wait!

I was going to give these moss treats to Slimy. Use them to lure him out!
He loves snacks!!!

Genius! One whiff and Slimy will come running!
Well, not *running*... but you know what I mean.

Just follow the goo, Iggy.
Don't let yourself get...
FWOOSH!

...terrified!

Calm down. Don't lose the trail.
Hurgh! I forget that Slimy can climb almost anything.

Oh no. Where did the trail go?

Here, Slimy! I have tasty moss snacks!

Slimy?
RRRRRRRRR!

RRRIIBBIT!
WHAAA!
PLOP
Uh... do you want some tasty moss?
I promise I'm not tasty at all.
FWIPP!
EEK!

GULP!
Oh! Haha! Glad you liked it!
Hey, toad buddy, maybe you can help me.
Have you seen a snail around here?

nod

That way? Can you show me—

Well... nice to meet you! Thanks for the tip!
JUMP!

Yes! The trail *does* pick up over here!

It sure was silly of me to get so startled. She was a perfectly polite toad.

But I gave her *all* the moss. Argh!

I'll just have to find Slimy on my own. Before anything else does!

Aha! Slimy's chew-goo!
And the goo is fresh!

He's got to be close!
Ouch!
thunk

Uh-oh. The trail goes right up the rock!

It's too smooth for me to climb, but there must be some other way up.

Think, Iggy, think.
SNIFF
GAH!

Remember, Iggy. Big, scary animals aren't always *actually* scary.

Hello there! Have, um, *you* seen a snail around here?

...

Yip!

You—you want me to climb on your back?

Can you bring me to Slimy?

Whoa!
Hnngh! You're a... little faster... than Slimy!

SNIFF
SNIFF
SSKKID!
WHA!
Phew! You gotta warn me before you—

Slimy!

You're okay!

I was so scared you'd be lost forever.
But I should've known you'd just go after your favorite food.

Thanks for your help.

Y'know, I thought I lost a friend today, Slimy.
But turns out I might have found a few new ones!

Kora will worry if we're not back soon.
Should we grab snacks for the road?
nod
In fact... I know how to make the return trip a little faster.
Giddy up, buddy! Follow the 'shroom and we'll be home in no time.

Woo-hoo! Now we're cruising!
Of course, we could've asked the fox for a lift.
But I don't think he wants snail goo in his fur.

At Iggy's house . . .
I should've gone with Iggy.
Who knows what kind of big, hungry animals he ran into?
Oh, I met a couple! I'll tell you all about them later, Kora.
Iggy! Slimy! You're back!

Turns out Slimy can wander pretty far when he's hungry.
And he's *always* hungry.
That's why I'll be planting some mushrooms *much* closer to home.

Because the next time Slimy wants an adventure?
We're all going together!
THE END

TAKING A CLOSER LOOK

1. Slimy gets loose because Iggy didn't close the gate quite right. Think of a time when you made a mistake because you were in a hurry. What did you learn from that mistake?

2. The woods are an important setting in the story. How would you describe them? What in the art and text makes you think that?

3. Iggy is afraid of both the toad and fox at first, but then he learns that they're kind and helpful. Have you ever made an assumption about someone or something that turned out not to be true? What changed your mind?

4. How do you think Slimy's journey through the woods went? Did he meet any animals? Did he face any challenges? Write his story! If you'd like, draw panels to go with it.

THE WRITER

Steve Foxe is the Eisner and Ringo Award-nominated author of more than 75 comics and children's books. He has written for properties like Spider-Man, Pokémon, Mario, LEGO City, Batman, Justice League, Baby Shark, and more. He lives somewhere cold with his partner and their dog, which he never lets out of his sight.

THE ARTIST

Daniela Barros is a Portuguese illustrator and comic artist. Inspired by manga but with a colorful style all her own, Daniela works her magic for publishing houses across the world, creating imagery full of fantasy, charm, and intrigue. She has illustrated for Scholastic, Chiado Books, PublishWay, Midori Editora, and Rebel Studio board games.

READ THEM ALL!

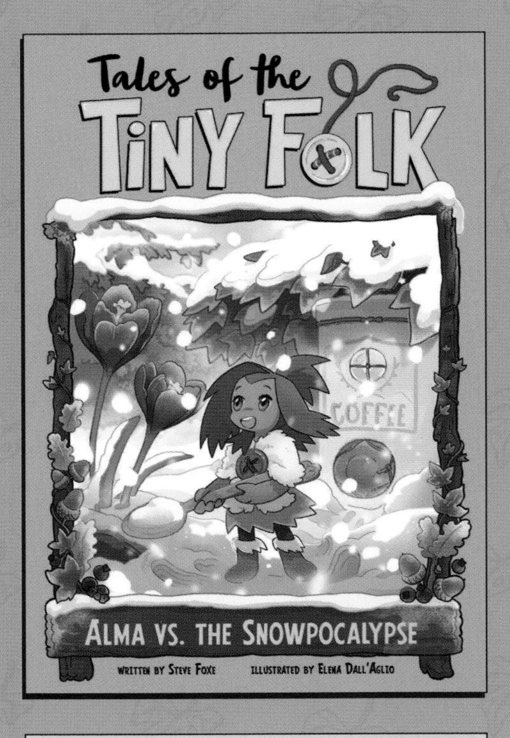

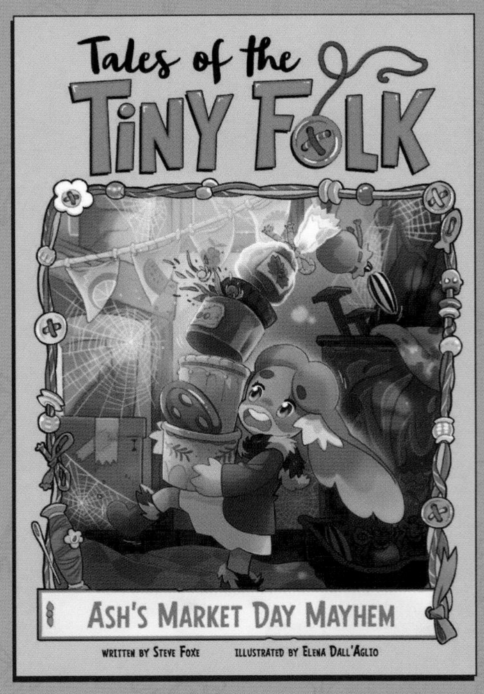

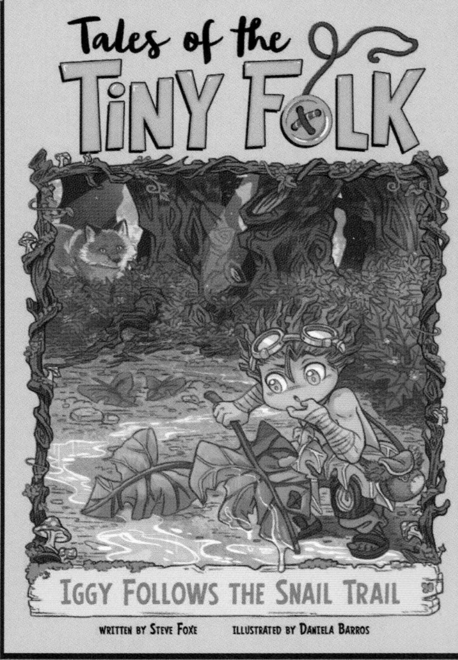

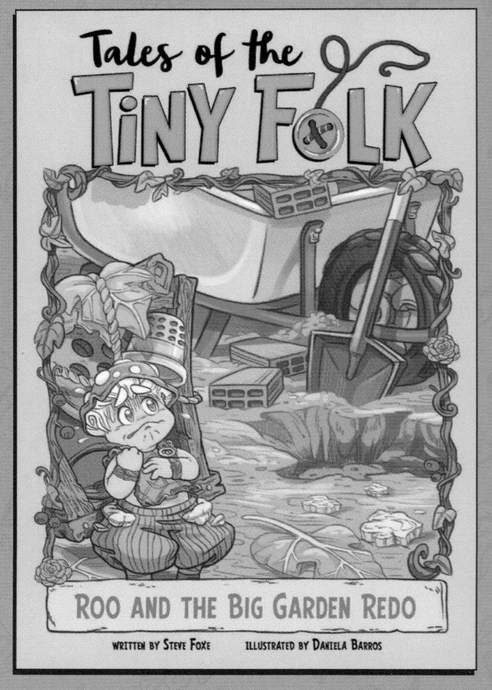